TJ Zaps the New Kid
Stopping a Social Bully

HA HA HA HA HA HA HA

BOOK 1

written by
Lisa Mullarkey

illustrated by
Gary LaCoste

visit us at www.abdopublishing.com

In memory of Bruce Berman. Miss you . . . —LM
For Ashley —GL

Published by Magic Wagon, a division of the ABDO Group,
PO Box 398166, Minneapolis, MN 55439. Copyright © 2013 by
Abdo Consulting Group, Inc. International copyrights reserved
in all countries. All rights reserved. No part of this book may
be reproduced in any form without written permission from the
publisher.

Calico Chapter Books™ is a trademark and logo of Magic Wagon.

Printed in the United States of America, North Mankato, Minnesota.
052012
092012
This book contains at least 10% recycled materials.

Text by Lisa Mullarkey
Illustrations by Gary LaCoste
Edited by Stephanie Hedlund and Rochelle Baltzer
Cover and interior design by Neil Klinepier

Library of Congress Cataloging-in-Publication Data
Mullarkey, Lisa.
   TJ zaps the new kid : stopping a social bully / by Lisa Mullarkey ;
illustrated by Gary LaCoste.
       p. cm. -- (TJ Trapper, bully zapper ; bk. 1)
   Summary: Livvy, the new girl at school, is a bully who ridicules the
other children, and it is up to TJ and his guidance counselor father
to work out a strategy that will improve her behavior--and save TJ's
birthday party.
   ISBN 978-1-61641-905-9
   1. Bullying--Juvenile fiction. 2. Schools--Juvenile fiction. 3.
Birthday parties--Juvenile fiction. [1. Bullies--Fiction. 2. Schools--
Fiction. 3. Birthday parties--Fiction.] I. LaCoste, Gary, ill. II. Title.
   PZ7.M91148Tjn 2012
   813.6--dc23   2012007919

Contents

Livvy Armstrong

The second Livvy Armstrong opened her mouth, I knew she was trouble.

"Salutations, class," said Livvy. When no one answered back, she rolled her eyes and added, "That means hello."

Ms. Perry rushed over to her. "You must be Livvy. Welcome! The kids are excited to meet you."

"Of course they are," said Livvy.

Ms. Perry frowned.

"Just kidding," said Livvy. "I'm excited, too."

Ms. Perry sighed. "Well, I hope so." Then she pointed to the empty seat near me. "You'll sit there."

I waved. "Hi! I'm TJ Trapper."

Livvy plunked her backpack on the desk and ignored me.

I waved again.

She still ignored me.

I tried again. "Um . . . salutations?"

Livvy looked up, but not at me, and smiled. "Oh, salutations!"

She was looking at Maxi Weber, who was bouncing over to our desks.

"Your dress is nice," said Maxi from behind thick glasses. "You look so pretty."

Livvy took one look at Maxi's clothes and turned her nose up in the air. "I'd never be allowed to wear ripped jeans to school. But you look very interesting in those grubby pants."

Maxi's face turned as red as the polish on Livvy's nails. "Grubby?"

"Just kidding," said Livvy. "I wish my mom would let me wear tattered clothes.

They're . . . interesting." Then she looked at me. "*Tattered* means ripped and torn, you know."

She grabbed Maxi's hand. "I think that girls who wear tattered clothes must have very exciting lives. I bet you have lots of fun adventures. Maybe we'll have adventures together!"

Maxi nodded as she tried to stretch her shirt to cover the holes. "They ripped on the playground this morning." Then she frowned. "They are kind of ugly, I guess."

"Don't forget what Ms. Perry said about your jeans last week, Maxi," I said.

Maxi smiled. "Oh yeah! She said she'd want jeans just like mine if she was in fourth grade." She pointed to her pockets. "She likes my sparkly hearts."

Livvy folded her arms and declared, "She lied."

"That wasn't very nice," I said.

"I was just kidding," said Livvy, patting Maxi on the back. "Why, I bet you didn't rip them just going down a slide anyway. You were probably trying to escape the jaws of a T. rex or running away from a bank robber. Am I right?"

"It was a bank robber with bad breath," said Maxi, waving her hand in front of her nose. "Stiiiink-y!"

Livvy laughed. "Aren't you clever?" Then she leaned closer to Maxi and whispered. "Maybe it was just DJ that you smelled."

I made a face at her. "Well, I like Maxi's pants."

Livvy glared at me. "Listen, RJ . . ."

"It's TJ," I said.

"It's just that I like to be neat and clean," she said. She stared at the green streaks on my sleeve. "Obviously, you don't."

"They're grass stains," I said. "From football."

Livvy smirked. "If you say so."

Maxi bit her lip when she looked at her jeans again. "I forgot to wash my good dress last night." She shrugged. "My bad."

I've known Maxi since kindergarten. She'd rather eat a bowl of bugs than wear a dress.

Then Maxi's eyes lit up. "But it got dirty after I climbed back into the castle after I slayed the dragon."

Livvy's eyes grew wide. "You're so brave, Maxi! I knew you'd only wear tattered clothes if your good dress was dirty. I just knew it."

"Hey," I said to Livvy, "what's your problem? Who cares what she's wearing? Pick on someone your own . . ."

"Size?" said Livvy. "Don't be mean, DJ!" Then she dropped her voice to a loud whisper. "Though, Maxi, you really are the shortest girl I've ever seen in fourth grade. Shouldn't your name be Mini?" Livvy laughed. "You're adorable." She pinched Maxi's cheeks. "You're like a cute puppy dog, Mini."

Maxi smiled. "Thanks." Then she added, "I think."

"Her name is Maxi," I said. "Don't call her *Mini*."

"Geez, I'm *just* kidding," Livvy said. "What does *TJ* stand for anyway?"

"It doesn't stand for anything," I said. "It's just TJ."

Livvy frowned. "It must stand for *something*." She leaned over to put a notebook inside her desk. That's when she saw the inside of mine. "What a mess!" she shrieked. "I know what *TJ* stands for: Too Junky! Just like your desk."

Before I could say anything, she winked. "*Just kidding.*"

"I knew you were kidding," said Maxi, standing on her tiptoes. Even on her toes, she was still the shortest kid in the class. Maybe even the whole school.

I clenched my jaw and walked away. I had better things to do. Like pass out my birthday invitations!

I walked to the mailboxes and started to toss invitations into each one.

"Do you have one for everyone?" asked Ms. Perry from her desk. "You know the rule, TJ. Unless you have one for everyone—"

I waved the rest of the envelopes in the air. "I even brought an extra for Livvy."

Livvy rushed over to me. "*You* have something for *me*, DJ? How wonderful!"

"*TJ*," I muttered. "My name is TJ." I held out the envelope. "It's an invitation to my party."

Livvy jumped up and down. "A party? I love social gatherings! I'll buy a new dress!" She snatched an envelope out of my hand.

Ethan had just finished copying his homework off of the board. "You have to wear jeans and boots to TJ's party. We milk cows, ride horses, and have a tug-of-war contest over the mud pit. It's awesome."

Livvy scrunched her face. "Mud pit? Ponies?" She tore open the envelope and read the invitation. "Farms are *so* first grade, don't you think?" Then she laughed.

"It's juvenile," she said. "*Juvenile* means babyish, you know." Then she giggled. "*TJ*. Too Juvenile! Get it, TJ?"

"My parties aren't babyish," I said.

Livvy handed the invitation back to me. She pretended a shiver ran up her spine. "I bet you have clowns, too."

I folded my arms. "But my clowns juggle fire sticks!"

Livvy wasn't listening. "I can't go to a *baby* party. I won't."

I waited for her to say, "Just kidding." But she didn't.

I glared at Livvy Armstrong.

She wasn't just trouble, she was a party pooper, too.

The Point and Laugh

During recess, I noticed a bunch of girls looking at me while I was playing football. Every once in a while, Livvy would stop talking and point to me. The whole group would burst out laughing a few seconds later.

What's she up to? I wondered as I threw the ball to Ethan. *Out of all the new kids we could have gotten, we got stuck with Livvy Armstrong.*

I tried to ignore the girls but I couldn't. Every time I'd get within twenty feet of them, they'd laugh. It made me want to run all the way home.

What were they laughing at? Was my zipper down? Did my underwear stick out of my jeans? Was someone making bunny ears behind me again? I had to find out.

When Ethan threw the football to me, I missed it on purpose. It sailed over my head and landed near Kelli's foot.

I ran over to get it. "What are you guys doing?"

"Guys?" shrieked Livvy. "We're not *guys*! Do we look like *guys*?"

Everyone cracked up. "It wasn't that funny," I said.

But I guess it was because they started to laugh even harder.

"We were just talking about your party, DJ," said Livvy.

"It's TJ," said Maxi.

"Right, right. TJ. I must remember those initials. TJ. RJ. PJ. DJ. They all sound so much alike," said Livvy. "Anyway, we were talking about your party. You know, the one at the farm. With the ponies and clowns."

"You may think the party is for babies," I said. "But it's not. Everyone always has fun. And I'm not having ponies. They're horses and we get to ride them."

"I always have fun," said Maxi. "We all do."

Everyone else nodded.

"And they aren't just clowns," I said. "They perform magic. And they juggle all sorts of things. Dangerous things."

"Right," Livvy said, grinning. "Giddyap, little fella!"

The girls thought Livvy was a barrel of laughs. They laughed so hard when she said *giddyap* that Kelli started to cough. My face burned.

"Come on, TJ," yelled Ethan as he jumped up and down. "Throw the ball back."

"Go play your little game," said Livvy. "You look so cute missing all those catches."

Everyone laughed again.

"*Just kidding*," said Livvy. Then she got serious. "You know I'm only kidding. Right?"

My face got even hotter.

"I didn't miss *that* many," I said. "It was like one. Maybe two or three."

"He can count!" shouted Livvy. "The little cowboy can count! I've heard horses can count by tapping their hooves on the ground. Looks like one of the ponies is a good teacher."

I picked up the ball and threw it as far as I could. It soared over Ethan's head. "Why are you so mean?" I asked.

Livvy clutched her chest. "Mean? You think I'm mean? I'm only kidding with you. You can't take a little joke, can you?"

Then she rolled her eyes and looked up at the sky. "Oh, that's right. Babies can't take jokes." She looked at Maxi. "My bad."

Everyone but Maxi laughed. Now Maxi's face was as red as mine.

I went back to playing football, but I missed every single pass after that. I couldn't concentrate. My stomach hurt. When the bell rang to go back inside, I was the first one in line.

After recess, we always have math. Ms. Perry walked around and passed out the quizzes from the week before. When Ethan saw my 98, he said, "Hey, brainiac, that's like an F for you."

"Be quiet," I said. "It's not funny."

"Whoa!" said Ethan. "What's wrong with you? It was just a joke. You still got an A but you usually get a 100. Get it? I didn't mean anything by it."

I glanced at the clock. This day felt like it would never end. "Sorry, Ethan." Then I smiled so he'd know I wasn't mad.

But I wasn't smiling on the inside. I was thinking about Livvy. Thinking about the whole day. *What if I really couldn't take a joke? What if I really was acting like a baby? Maybe my party was babyish. Could Livvy be right?* I crumpled up my quiz and shoved it inside my desk.

But I didn't have time to think too much about it. Because just then, Maxi walked by and dropped a note on my desk.

After making sure Ms. Perry wasn't looking, I read it.

"Dear TJ, I just opened your invitation. I can't come to your party. I wish I could but I can't. Sorry. Double sorry. From Maxi." She drew a cake with ten candles on top. She dotted the *i* in her name with a smiley face.

When I looked at Maxi, she was sitting with Livvy in the math center. "Sorry," she mouthed. Then she shrugged her shoulders and started to work.

Maxi had never missed any of my parties before. I glared at Livvy. It was all her fault.

I looked at the candles on the top of Maxi's cake and slid down in my seat. I knew exactly what I'd be wishing for on Saturday.

Dad Knows Best

When the bus stopped in front of my house, I jumped off and ran up the steps. I knew Auntie Stella would be waiting in the kitchen with a snack.

"How was school, kiddo?" asked Auntie Stella. She held out a plate of Crispy Treats. I scooped up three.

She narrowed her eyes and smiled. "As long as you don't tell your father."

"Aren't you having any?" I asked before I stuffed one in my mouth.

She patted her stomach. "You know me, kiddo. I've been picking at them all day. Let's just say I've had . . . well, let's not say it!" She kissed my cheek. I rubbed at it.

I'd told Auntie Stella a million times that I was too old for lipstick kisses but she always laughed. "You're never too old for Auntie Stella's love," she said.

Auntie Stella isn't my real aunt. But she's been helping my dad take care of me ever since I was born. Dad always says we can't live without her and she can't live without us. I think he's right. Even though I call her Auntie Stella, everyone thinks she's my grandmother.

"So how was your day?" asked Auntie Stella. "Did you pass out the invitations?"

Just then the back door slammed. "Hey, champ," said Dad. "How ya doing, buddy?"

He opened his mouth just in time for Auntie Stella to shove a Crispy Treat inside. "Ow ah oo, Sella?"

Auntie Stella laughed. "Same as always. Busy! Busy washing. Busy cleaning. Busy cooking. Busy planning parties. What would you two do without me?"

"We have no idea. Do we, champ?" asked Dad.

I took another treat. "Nope." Sitting around the table after school with them was usually my favorite part of the day. But as soon as Auntie Stella mentioned the party, I wanted to run away.

Auntie Stella slid Dad a glass of water. He took a long sip. "Your best yet, Stella."

She smacked him with the dish towel. "Oh, you!"

"About the party, Auntie Stella," I said as I looked down at my napkin. "I'm thinking of maybe, you know, changing it. I don't think I want to go to the farm this year."

Auntie Stella lifted my chin up. "Really? You've been bugging me to book the farm all week. Yesterday you were excited. What's going on?"

I took a deep breath as I thought about Livvy. "Maybe I should go to laser tag instead. The farm is kind of babyish . . . don't you think?"

Dad shrugged. "It's up to you, buddy. But didn't you say everyone does the laser tag thing?"

Auntie Stella interrupted. "Babyish? Who's been feeding you that nonsense?" Then she ripped off her apron. "Spill it, buster. You're not telling us something."

Auntie Stella knew *everything*. It could be so annoying. It was like she had a crystal ball.

Dad's eyes lit up. "I almost forgot! How was the new girl? Is it Olivia?"

I nodded. "Livvy. And she's mean. Meaner than Timmy Price."

Dad looked horrified. "Meaner than Timmy Price? Impossible!"

Timmy Price was a kid my dad knew in eighth grade. He used to steal everyone's lunch money. If you didn't have any, he'd take your lunch and squish it in his hands.

"Is this Livvy mean to *you*?" asked Auntie Stella. "If she is, I'll give her the old dish towel." She snapped the towel in the air.

Dad laughed.

Auntie Stella didn't. "Wait a second. Does this Livvy girl have anything to do with you suddenly wanting a laser tag party?"

She always knows! "Not really."

"Aha!" said Auntie Stella. "*Not really* means *yes*. Spill it," she repeated.

So I did. "She's mean to Maxi but it's like Maxi doesn't even realize it. But she's extra mean to me. I don't know why. I didn't do anything but say hi."

I tore my napkin into small pieces. "She's just not nice. She keeps saying all this stuff to me. Then she says *just kidding*. But I know she's not."

"Oh no," said Dad. "She's one of *those*."

"One of those *whats*?" asked Auntie Stella.

Dad leaned back in his chair and put his hands behind his head. "What exactly did Livvy do?"

Dad is a guidance counselor at the high school in town. He always asks questions about the kids in my class.

So I told Dad and Auntie Stella all about Livvy Armstrong. When I finished, Dad sighed and rubbed his temple.

"Well, champ," Dad said, "you're right. Livvy is mean."

"And she's definitely a party pooper," said Auntie Stella.

"But she's also something else," said Dad. "Something much worse."

"What?" asked Auntie Stella, leaning forward.

Dad looked me straight in the eye. "You know what she is, buddy. Don't you?"

I nodded. "Yep." I thought of Timmy Price. "Livvy Armstrong is a bully."

Big time.

How to Handle a Bully

"Ignore her," said Auntie Stella. "Treat her like she treats you."

Dad shook his head. "That's not the best plan, Stella. First of all, if TJ treats her the same way, then *he'd* be bullying *her*. Two wrongs don't make a right."

Auntie Stella threw her hands into the air. "Then ignore her. Pretend she's not there."

"That usually doesn't work either," said Dad. "A bully gets angrier when they're being ignored. She'll just work harder to get a rise out of TJ."

"I'm surprised a girl would bully a boy," said Auntie Stella. "She's so young. Too young to bully, isn't she?"

Dad shook his head. "Bullies come in all shapes and sizes. It doesn't matter how a person looks or how old they are. Even adults can be bullies." Then he lowered his voice and looked at Auntie Stella. "We know that, don't we?" He looked sad for a second. I'm pretty sure he was thinking about my mom.

"Then what should I do?" I asked.

"Well, the good news is that you already did the best thing you could do," said Dad. "You told us—adults. So many kids try to deal with a bully alone. They're too embarrassed or scared to tell an adult. But getting an adult involved helps."

Dad chewed on his lip. He did that whenever he was trying to decide what to do next. "There's a chance she'll be nicer tomorrow. She could have had a case of first-day jitters. Maybe she thought she could fit in better by joking around a lot. Not that it makes her behavior acceptable. She needs to know that if her jokes make anyone feel bad or uncomfortable, then they aren't funny."

He loosened his tie. "I'm glad you told me, TJ. Maybe we can stop her bullying before it gets worse. If it continues, we'll need to tell Ms. Perry."

"No way," I said. "Ms. Perry hates tattletales. She'll be mad. There's no way I'm saying a word."

"But you wouldn't be tattling," said Dad. "I always tell my students that if someone's hurting them or making them or someone else feel bad or uncomfortable, they need to report it. So, we call it reporting. Reporting is a lot different than tattling."

I didn't really believe him. "Are you sure?"

"Sadly, I deal with this kind of thing all the time. Trust me. Kids who tattle want to get other kids in trouble. They think it's fun to see someone get punished. Usually, they tattle about something that doesn't even involve them. But reporting is when you tell an adult because you want to help someone or yourself get out of trouble."

"Now I get it," I said. I felt a little better. But I was still worried the kids would think I was a tattletale.

"Let's see what tomorrow brings. If she picks on you or anyone else, you'll need a plan. It depends on who the target is."

"What do you mean?" I asked. "Like target practice?"

"Sort of," said Dad. "Bullies zero in on a kid that they want to pick on. That's their target. They'll pick on the target, make fun of the target, make the target feel bad about himself. Bullies can make life pretty miserable for the target. You get the idea."

Auntie Stella hugged me. "I still say we should snap her with the dish towel."

"There won't be any snapping of towels," said Dad. He tried to act serious but finally cracked up.

Then he got up and grabbed paper and a pencil. "Let's think about Livvy and her teasing. If she does it tomorrow, try to change the subject." He wrote *Change Subject* on the first line. "Catch her off guard. Ask her about her old school. Ask her questions about herself."

"That could work," I said. "She loves to talk about herself."

"Sometimes asking why helps," said Dad. He wrote *Why* on the second line. "Bullies often don't know why they say something. They get tongue-tied and might walk away when challenged. If she calls you a baby for liking the farm, say, '*Why* am I a baby?' If she says, 'Clowns are stupid,' ask her why. Bullies usually don't have answers. They only have insults."

Dad made it sound so easy. But I knew it couldn't be. Could it? "I still want to call the farm and cancel. I think we should go to the laser tag place."

Dad interrupted. "Bullies also try to

make the target think they did something wrong or that something is wrong with them. Your party is an example. Don't second-guess yourself, TJ. The farm is a place you love. Don't let Livvy make you think it's babyish."

That was easy for him to say. I grabbed my backpack. "I better start my homework. Thanks, Dad. Thanks, Auntie Stella."

Auntie Stella leaned over and whispered, "Just say the word, TJ." Then she snapped the towel in the air again. I laughed.

Dad took another sip of water. "I'm glad you told me all of this, TJ. We'll put an end to it before it gets worse. I promise. Today she picked on you and Maxi. Who knows who will become her target tomorrow."

My throat felt lumpy. I didn't want Livvy to bully anyone else. So, I knew exactly what I had to do.

Today, she met TJ Trapper.

Tomorrow, I'd introduce her to TJ Trapper, Bully Zapper.

Name-calling Again

When Livvy saw me the next day, she waved. "Salutations, RJ."

"It's TJ," I said. Then I thought of Dad's advice. "How do you like our school so far? What was your last school like?"

Livvy clicked her tongue and raised her right eyebrow. "I miss my friends. I hope they can visit. My parents said they could, but we moved so far away."

She looked at Ms. Perry. "I miss my teacher, too. Maxi is nice. So is Kelli. And you're okay, RJ." Then she put her hand up to her mouth. "Oops. Did I get your name wrong again?"

"That's okay," I lied. "You can call me RJ, DJ, PJ, or MJ. Whatever you want. I like it. It sounds kind of cool."

"It does?" asked Livvy. She bit her lip. "You mean you *like* when I mess up your name?"

I nodded. "Well, I feel bad for you that you can't remember it. Sometimes my mind can't remember facts either. So, any name is okay."

Livvy put her hands on her hips. "TJ Trapper! My memory is fine." Then she huffed. "And if I remember correctly, I'm not coming to your party because it's a *baby* party."

I was ready for the baby party stuff.

"Yep," I said. "You do have a good memory. You did say it's a baby party." Then I pretended I was confused. "*Why* is it a baby party?"

"The ponies and clowns," said Livvy. "Now who has a bad memory?"

"Ah," I said, "that's right. So what else makes it a baby party? Is it when we make the apple cider doughnuts?"

Livvy licked her lips. "Do you use real apples?"

I nodded. "And cider."

Livvy tilted her head and looked like she was trying to think of something else to say.

"What else makes it a baby party?" I asked. "Is it the gigantic corn maze we have to go through? The theme is a rocket blasting into space this year. We have to go through all the planets if we want to get out. It's the hardest one they've ever had."

Livvy shrugged, but she didn't say a word.

"Anything wrong, Livvy?" asked Ms. Perry.

Livvy looked down at her desk. "No, Ms. Perry. TJ is just telling me about his party."

She got my name right!

Then Maxi walked over to our desks. She was wearing a dress!

"Maxi, I like your dress!" said Livvy. "It's so pretty!"

Maxi beamed. "Thanks! My mom finally washed it." She spun around on one foot.

Then Kelli walked over.

"Hi, Kelli Belly," said Livvy.

"Hi, Livvy Pivvy," said Kelli. "Hi, Maxi Faxi." They burst out laughing and rushed over to the rug with their journals.

Ethan called me over.

"What, Ethan Beethan?" I said.

"Huh?" said Ethan.

I shook my head. "Nothing. Forget it."

Ethan started to read his journal entry to me. It was all about my party last year, but I couldn't concentrate on what he was saying.

Why not? Because I was listening to Livvy. I could tell she had picked another target—Kelli.

"Why aren't you wearing a dress, Kelli?" asked Livvy. Then she stared at Kelli's pants. "Aren't those the same jeans you wore yesterday?"

Kelli picked a piece of lint off of her knee. "My mom said I should wear my pants three times before washing them. Unless they get dirty."

Livvy put her hands on her cheeks. "You wear dirty pants to school? That's gross!" Then she turned to Maxi. "We should call her *Smelly Kelli*."

Kelli's face squished up. "I don't smell."

"Smelly Kelli, Smelly Kelli," Livvy sang.

Kelli's eyes filled up with tears. "Stop calling me Smelly Kelli. I'm telling my mom."

Kelli's voice cracked. I could tell she was about to cry.

"Just kidding," said Livvy. Then she rolled her eyes. "But wearing something

three times is just gross! Smelly Kelli gross."

Kelli whined. "Stop making fun of me."

"Sorrrrrrryyyyyyy," said Livvy. "I was only kidding. Can't you take a joke?"

But I could tell she wasn't kidding. And she definitely wasn't sorry. She had a smirk on her face. She looked like she was glad she made someone cry.

I took Dad's advice. I knew what I had to do. I was TJ Trapper and I was going to be a bully zapper.

I walked up to Ms. Perry. "Can I talk to you privately, please?"

She was grading papers. "What is it, TJ? Is someone bleeding? Because if they're not, I shouldn't be disturbed."

"No one's bleeding," I said. "But . . ."

She put her marker down. "But what?"

"Livvy's being mean to Kelli. She said—"

Ms. Perry stopped me. "You know how I feel about tattling, TJ. I don't want to hear it. Let Kelli and Livvy work it out themselves."

"But, you don't understand," I said.

Ms. Perry stood up. "No, TJ. You don't understand. No tattling. You're in fourth grade." She pointed to my seat.

I slowly walked back to my desk. My own teacher didn't know the difference between tattling and reporting.

I wanted to zap the bully. Instead, I got zapped.

Where's a dish towel when you need one?

Reporting . . . Not Tattling

Dad didn't get home until Auntie Stella had dinner on the table. "How did it go today, buddy?" he asked as soon as he sat down.

"I asked him the same thing," said Auntie Stella. "But he didn't feel like talking."

"That's because I heard the answering machine when I got home. Three more girls aren't coming to my party." Then I slammed my fist down on the table. "Thanks, Livvy!"

"Are you sure Livvy's to blame?" asked Dad.

"Positive," I said. "She keeps telling everyone in the class that my party is for babies." I flicked a crumb off of the table. "I did what you said today. I changed the subject when Livvy started to tease me and then I kept asking her why. It worked."

"That's great," said Dad. "But why don't you look happier?"

"Because Livvy found a new target," I said. "She teased Kelli about wearing dirty clothes. Then she called her a mean name. She kept calling her Smelly Kelli even when Kelli told her it wasn't funny. Livvy said she was just kidding but I could tell she wasn't."

"That's what bullies do," said Dad. "They think if they say *just kidding,* it's okay. They hide behind those words."

"So I thought about what you said about reporting. When I saw Kelli start to cry, I tried to tell Ms. Perry."

"That's great," said Dad.

"That's my boy," said Auntie Stella.

"No, it wasn't a good idea. It was a terrible idea!" I said. "Ms. Perry wouldn't let me tell her. She said I was tattling and sent me back to my seat."

Dad looked angry. "Did you tell her you were reporting?"

I let out a huge sigh. "Dad, you're a guidance counselor. You know about reporting. She called it tattling and got mad at me."

"Explain it to her," said Auntie Stella. "Set her straight."

"He shouldn't have to," said Dad. "Teachers should know the difference, or at least be willing to listen to their students. We'll never solve bully problems unless everyone's on board. If we don't stop the bullying in the younger grades, those bullies come to high school and are meaner than ever."

Dad grabbed the piece of paper from the day before. "I'm glad you used these two strategies. But here's something I should have told you about yesterday." He wrote *Bystander* on the third line. Then he wrote: *Speak Up* next to it.

"When you heard Livvy tease Kelli, did you say anything?" he asked.

"Not really," I said. "But when she teased Maxi yesterday, I told her to knock it off and she did. At least for a little while."

"That's good, TJ. Lots of times, if the people that witness the bullying speak up, they can stop the bullying. Bystanders are the people who see and hear the bully picking on a target but don't do anything," Dad explained.

"Sometimes bystanders join in and tease the target, too. Sometimes they walk away

How to handle
a Bully
* Change Subject
* Why
* Bystander:
  Speak Up

because they don't want to get involved. But what really makes a difference is when the bystander does something. When they jump in and help the kid being bullied they become an upstander."

"How?" I asked. "What can a fourth grader do?"

"More than you think," said Dad. "If you don't do anything, then what will happen?"

I shrugged.

"I bet Livvy's teasing could get worse," said Auntie Stella. "Maybe kids would laugh at her jokes. Maybe some of those kids would become bullies too and start teasing Kelli."

"That's right," said Dad. "And that would encourage Livvy to tease Kelli even more in hopes she'd get more kids to laugh." Dad moved his chair closer to me. "But what would happen if you called Livvy out on it? What if you pointed out to everyone that she's bullying? Or if you told her it wasn't nice to tease kids?

"If you stand up to her, I bet some of your friends would, too," Dad continued. "When that happens, the bullying usually stops because the bully is getting attention they don't want. Try it next time."

Dad made it sound so easy. "I'll try anything," I said. "It's just that . . . Livvy is a bully, but the girls think she's funny."

"That may not last long," said Dad. "Bullies usually don't have many friends. If she continues to bully, she'll lose whatever friends she's making. She needs to learn that there are lots of ways to be funny without insulting someone. You don't need to be rude to be funny."

Dad bit his lip again. "I need to call Ms. Perry and talk to her."

"No way, Dad! She'll be mad at me for telling you!" I protested.

Auntie Stella rubbed my arm. "She won't be mad."

"I agree," said Dad. "She may be embarrassed, but I don't think she'll be mad. She wants the kids in her class to feel good about themselves and feel safe, doesn't she?"

I nodded.

"Well, when a bully is around, it's hard for kids to feel comfortable. They're too worried that they'll be the next target. I really think Ms. Perry needs to know about Livvy."

Dad could tell I was upset. He chewed on his lip some more and scratched his head. "How about I call Mrs. Morris first?" he finally suggested.

Mrs. Morris was our school's guidance counselor. "That would be better," I said. "Trust me, Dad. Ms. Perry really seemed mad at me."

"Then it's all settled," said Dad. "I'll call Mrs. Morris in the morning. In the meantime, take action. Stick up for the target. Be an upstander."

"Stick to the targets like glue," said Auntie Stella. "And make sure you don't become a target again."

I pretended to shoot a bow and arrow. "I will," I promised. "No one's going to use me for target practice again."

And I meant it.

Upstanding

When I got to school the next day, Ethan was showing Livvy something. "My tooth fell out last night. I found this dollar under my pillow this morning." He flashed her a smile. "Now I look like Fang Face."

Livvy took a closer look. "You do have fangs! You look like a vampire. Fang Face is a good name for you." She held out her hand. "Nice to meet you, Fang Face."

Ethan laughed and started talking like Dracula.

"How come you only got a dollar?" asked Livvy. "The tooth fairy leaves me at least five dollars every time I lose a tooth."

"Wow! You must be rich," said Ethan. "I wish I'd get five dollars."

Livvy opened her mouth like she was about to say something. But she snapped it shut.

Then Maxi skipped over to her. She was wearing pants again. "Where's your dress?" asked Livvy. "You look so much nicer when you wear a dress."

"It's dirty," said Maxi. "I spilled milk on it at dinner."

"What about your other dresses?" said Livvy.

"I only have one," said Maxi in a voice as small as her.

"One dress? Are you serious?" asked Livvy. "I never heard of a girl having only one dress. I have at least a hundred." Then she patted Maxi on the head. "Poor Mini is poor!"

"I'm not poor," said Maxi.

Livvy got down on her knees and clasped her hands together. "Ethan, please, please, please help Mini. She's poor. Give her your dollar. Her family needs it."

Maxi started to cry. "I'm not poor. And stop calling me *Mini*."

I handed her a tissue. "Good things come in small packages, Maxi." That's what Maxi always says to us.

Maxi tried to smile before she blew her nose. As Livvy stood up, she rolled her eyes at Maxi.

I turned to Livvy and said, "You're a bully. You say mean things to people but then you say *just kidding*. It's not funny. It's mean."

Livvy batted her eyelashes. "But I am just kidding. This school is full of babies. Big babies."

"I'm not a baby," I said. "Am I, Ethan?"

Ethan shook his head. "Nope. Neither are Maxi, Kelli, Lamar, or . . . anyone in our class." Then he added, "Except you, Livvy."

"No, Ethan. Livvy isn't a baby either." I remembered that Dad said not to bully back. "But she is a bully," I said. "And we don't want bullies in our class, do we?"

"I don't," said Maxi. Then she turned to Livvy. "I can't be friends with you if you pick on people."

"Me either," said Kelli. "When you called me Smelly Kelli, I got really mad. You didn't even care."

"I can't be friends with you either," said Ethan.

Livvy looked shocked. "But I never picked on you."

"But you're mean to my friends," said Ethan. "Why would I want to be friends with you when you don't like my friends?"

Livvy shook her fist at us. "Fine! I don't want to be friends with any of you either." Then she shook her fist right in front of my face. "That includes you, PJ."

Ms. Perry rushed over. "Livvy! Why are you shaking your fist? That's not very nice."

Livvy put her hand down. "They're bullying me, Ms. Perry. They called my dress ugly. They said I was poor. They keep making fun of my name." She pretended to wipe away a tear. "I wish I never moved here."

What a liar!

Ms. Perry hugged Livvy. "Oh, Livvy, I'm so sorry. I wasn't paying attention."

I could see a smirk on Livvy's face. Just then the classroom door opened. It was Mrs. Morris.

"May I see you for a minute, Ms. Perry?" Mrs. Morris asked.

Ms. Perry looked up. "I'm so glad you're here, Mrs. Morris. It seems like we have a little problem on our hands. I haven't sorted it all out yet but I think there's some bullying going on in here."

She looked at everyone on the carpet. "I'm upset that my students would bully anyone. Especially a new child."

Before I could say anything, Mrs. Morris did. "I'm going to talk to your entire class as soon as I can. But may I see you in the hallway now?"

Ms. Perry took a deep breath. "Back to your seats, kids."

We watched her as she went out into the hall. When she came back in, she looked miserable. She didn't say anything except, "Read a book at your seats. No talking."

It wasn't until lunch that we knew something was going on. That's when we saw Mrs. Morris come and get Livvy and her lunch tray. We didn't see Livvy for the rest of the day.

"Where do you think she is?" asked Ethan as we waited for the bus.

"Don't know. But I'm glad she wasn't at recess," I said. "She keeps telling kids not to come to my party when we're outside."

"She does?" asked Maxi.

I nodded. "That's why you and Kelli aren't coming, isn't it?"

Kelli laughed. "Is that what you thought? Troop 1023 has a Girl Scout meeting. We can't miss it. It's five of us in the class."

"So you don't think I'm having a baby party?"

"No way," said Maxi. "Your parties are the best."

"We don't want to miss it," said Kelli. "But it's at the same time as the meeting. There's nothing we can do."

I chewed on my lip just like my dad did. Finally, I said, "You're right. There's nothing you can do. But there's something *I* can do."

And I did it.

A Success After All!

"I'm so glad everyone's coming to your party today," said Auntie Stella. "Changing the time was a good idea. Now all the girls can come."

"Everyone but Livvy," I reminded her.

"Maybe that's for the best," said Dad. "If she really thinks it's a party for babies, she wouldn't enjoy herself." He took a sip of his coffee. "I wouldn't be surprised if there was more to it than that though."

"Whatever," I said. "I just can't wait. Are you sure we're making the apple cider doughnuts?"

"I double-checked yesterday," said Auntie Stella. "The kids can choose between making apple cider and pumpkin."

My stomach growled. "Yum!"

When we got to the farm to set up, there was already a car in the parking lot.

"Who's that?" asked Auntie Stella as she pressed her nose up to the window.

Dad strained his head. "I have no idea. It looks like a girl, TJ. Is she in your class?" He looked at the clock on the dashboard. "If it is, she's early."

I leaned forward and blinked twice. "It's Livvy!"

"Are you sure?" said Auntie Stella. "What's she doing here?"

Dad opened the door. "There's only one way to find out."

Livvy and her mom opened their doors at the same time. Livvy got out and stared at the ground. She was wearing a puffy dress and shiny shoes.

"You must be TJ," said Mrs. Armstrong. "Happy Birthday!"

Dad shook her hand and introduced himself and Auntie Stella.

Mrs. Armstrong spoke first. "Mrs. Morris told me you're a guidance counselor at the high school."

Dad nodded. "I've worked there for ten years. It's a great school district. I think you're going to like it here."

"I already do," said Mrs. Armstrong. "I've been worried about Livvy's bullying since first grade. But her last school told me that 'kids will be kids.' I knew there was a problem. I just didn't know what to do about it. Mrs. Morris promised me she'll help us."

Livvy kicked a pebble on the ground.

Dad glanced at me and Livvy. "Livvy, TJ would like you to stay at the party. Would you like to stay?"

"Not if I have to get on a horse. I'm afraid of them," said Livvy. "I don't want anyone to laugh at me."

"Never!" said Auntie Stella. "I won't go on them either. Last year, five kids decided not to ride. No one laughed at them."

KICK

"Really?" said Livvy. "Are you sure?"

I nodded. "They just made more doughnuts."

"And ate them," said Auntie Stella as she rubbed her stomach.

Dad chewed on his lip again. "Why doesn't Livvy help TJ and Auntie Stella set up? Then we can talk privately."

"Great idea," said Mrs. Armstrong. "Mrs. Morris filled me in on a lot of what's been happening. She said you're a great resource and I could learn a lot from you."

Livvy and her mom stayed for the whole party. When Kelli and Maxi saw them, they looked surprised.

"What are you doing here?" asked Maxi.

"I wanted to wish TJ a happy birthday," said Livvy.

"Don't you mean PJ? Or MJ?" asked Kelli.

"Nope," said Livvy. "TJ—I know his name. And I know yours, too," she said while looking at Maxi. "I won't ever call you Mini again. TJ was right. It was mean."

Maxi and Kelli whispered something to each other. Then Kelli held up a bag. "Your dress is really pretty. But . . ."

"But what?" asked Livvy.

"You might want to borrow these just in case you want to enter the tug-of-war contest," said Maxi.

Livvy peeked in the bag.

"We always bring extra clothes," said Kelli. "You can borrow them."

Four hours later, the party was over and we were back home.

"A success," said Auntie Stella. "I think everyone had a great time. Even Livvy."

I stood at attention and saluted them. "Thanks to me! I made Livvy stop bullying!"

Dad saluted me back. "Good job, TJ. But I wish I could say it was that easy. The truth is, Livvy bullies for a reason. She may not have bullied anyone today, but she could bully again tomorrow. Her mom said she's been bullying for a long time. It's hard to break the habit."

"Can she change?" asked Auntie Stella. "Or do I need to keep the old dish towel handy?"

"Anyone can change if they want to," said Dad. "It takes time, though. Mrs. Morris is going to work with Livvy. She's also going to start going into all of the classrooms to discuss bully behavior."

Then Dad patted my back.

"And Mrs. Morris is training the teachers to learn the difference between tattling and reporting."

That made me feel better!

"If she needs any help," I said, "you know who she can call, don't you?"

Dad pointed to himself. "Me?"

"Nope. Me," I said. "TJ Trapper, Bully Zapper."

The Bully Test

Have you ever been a bully? Ask yourself these questions.

 Do I like to leave others out to make them feel bad?

 Have I ever spread a rumor that I knew was not true?

 Do I like teasing others?

 Do I call others mean names to make myself feel better or get attention?

 Is it funny to me to see other kids getting made fun of?

If you answered yes to any of these questions, it's not too late to change. First, say "I'm sorry." And start treating others the way you want to be treated.

Be a Bully Zapper

A few tips on how to stop bullying that happens around you:

 Report bullying to an adult you trust. This is the most important thing you can do to stop bullying.

 Change the subject when a verbal bully starts bullying his or her target. This may distract him or her from bullying.

 Ask why a bully thinks a certain way. The bully will back down if he or she doesn't have a reason.

 Speak up for your friends. Bullies back down if they get attention they don't want.

Bullying Glossary

bystander - someone who watches but is not a part of a situation.

guidance counselor - a school worker who guides students in daily life.

ignore - to not pay attention to someone or something.

insult - a word or phrase that hurts a person's feelings.

reporting - telling an adult about being bullied.

social bullying - telling secrets, spreading rumors, giving mean looks, and leaving kids out on purpose.

target - someone marked for attack.

tattling - telling someone about another's actions in order to get him or her in trouble.

tease - to make fun of someone or something.

upstander - someone who sees bullying and stands up for the person being bullied.

verbal bullying - being mean to someone using words, such as by name-calling.

Further Reading

 Fox, Debbie. *Good-Bye Bully Machine.* Minneapolis: Free Spirit Publishing, 2009.

 Hall, Megan Kelley. *Dear Bully: Seventy Authors Tell Their Stories.* New York: HarperTeen, 2011.

 Romain, Trevor. *Bullies Are a Pain in the Brain.* Minneapolis: Free Spirit Publishing, 1997.

Web Sites

To learn more about bullying, visit ABDO Group online. Web sites about bullying are featured on our Book Links page. These links are routinely monitored and updated to provide the most current information available. **www.abdopublishing.com**

About the Author

Lisa Mullarkey is the author of the popular chapter book series, Katharine the Almost Great. She wears many hats: mom, teacher, librarian, and author. She is passionate about children's literature. She lives in New Jersey with her husband, John, and her children, Sarah and Matthew. She's happy to report that none of them are bullies.

About the Illustrator

Gary LaCoste began his illustration career 15 years ago. His clients included Hasbro, Nickelodeon, and Lego. Lately his focus has shifted to children's publishing, where he's enjoyed illustrating more than 25 titles. Gary happily lives in western Massachusetts with his wife, Miranda, and daughter, Ashley.